discard

The KidHaven Science Library

Diabetes

by Gail B. Stewart

KIDHAVEN
PRESS™

THOMSON
GALE

San Diego • Detroit • New York • San Francisco • Cleveland
New Haven, Conn. • Waterville, Maine • London • Munich

THOMSON
GALE

Cover Photo: © St. Bartholomew's Hospital/Science Source/Photo Researchers
© Lester V. Bergman/CORBIS, 16
Blackbirch Press, 20
© Children's Hospital & Medical Center/CORBIS, 37
© Corel Corporation, 21, 35
© Will & Deni McIntyre/Photo Researchers, 12, 28, 34
Brandy Noon, 7
© Richard T. Nowitz/CORBIS, 24
© Richard T. Nowitz/Science Source/Photo Researchers, 38
© Jose Luis Pelaez, Inc./CORBIS, 14
PhotoDisc, 5, 19, 26, 32, 39
© Michael Pole/CORBIS, 9
© Roger Ressmeyer/CORBIS, 30

© 2003 by KidHaven Press. KidHaven Press is an imprint of The Gale Group, Inc., a division of Thomson Learning, Inc.

KidHaven™ and Thomson Learning™ are trademarks used herein under license.

For more information, contact
KidHaven Press
27500 Drake Rd.
Farmington Hills, MI 48331-3535
Or you can visit our Internet site at http://www.gale.com

LIBRARY OF CONGRESS CATALOGING-IN-PUBLICATION DATA

Stewart, Gail, B. 1949–
    Diabetes / by Gail B. Stewart.
        p. cm. — (The KidHaven science library)
    Includes index.
    Summary: Discusses the early detection of diabetes, its symptoms, treatment, daily life with diabetes, and hope for the future.
    ISBN 0-7377-1013-6 (hardback : alk. paper)
    1. Diabetes—Juvenile literature. [1. Diabetes. 2. Diseases.] I. Title.II. Series.
    RC660.5 .S74 2003
    616.4'62—dc21
                                          2002013063

Printed in the United States of America

Contents

Chapter 1

What Is Diabetes?

For centuries people were puzzled by a strange disease. In ancient Greece, doctors gave the disease the name **diabetes**, a word meaning "passing through." That seemed to be one of the most obvious **symptoms** of the disease—a lot of **urine** passing through a patient's body very quickly. People with the disease were also weak and sick. And because doctors did not know how to treat diabetes, these patients almost always died.

Glucose

Today doctors know much more about this disease. Diabetes is a disease that interferes with the body's ability to change food into energy. Everyone knows that people need food for energy. People who have no energy cannot play sports. They cannot walk or ride a bicycle. Without energy, a person cannot even sleep or think. Everything people do depends on energy.

The foods people eat do not supply energy right away. First, the body must digest the food, breaking

Skateboarding, bicycling, and other activities require energy. Energy comes from food.

it down into tiny pieces. The body changes a lot of these pieces into a type of sugar called **glucose**. Glucose is an important fuel for a human body. It gives the body the energy it needs. After the food is changed into glucose, the bloodstream carries the glucose to each **cell**.

However, each little cell has a tough, protective wall around it. To get past the cell wall, the glucose needs some help. In a healthy body, glucose gets help from another substance, called **insulin**.

The Key

Insulin is made in a tongue-shaped organ called the **pancreas**, which is behind the stomach. After a person eats food and the body starts changing the food into glucose, the pancreas gets a signal. The signal alerts the pancreas to make more insulin. The more glucose traveling in the bloodstream, the more insulin is needed. Doctors say that insulin is like a key that helps the glucose get into the cells, where it is needed.

"It is an amazing system," says one medical student. "It goes on all of the time, and none of us is aware of it. Little signals passing within our bodies— various parts telling one another what's needed. The more you learn about the body, the more amazing it seems."[1]

But diabetes interferes with this process. The pancreas produces too little insulin, or none at all.

The Pancreas

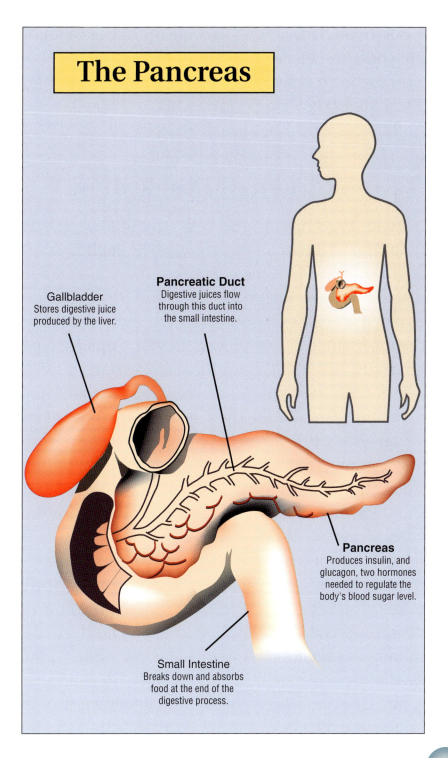

Gallbladder
Stores digestive juice produced by the liver.

Pancreatic Duct
Digestive juices flow through this duct into the small intestine.

Pancreas
Produces insulin, and glucagon, two hormones needed to regulate the body's blood sugar level.

Small Intestine
Breaks down and absorbs food at the end of the digestive process.

Sometimes people with diabetes produce insulin, but their bodies do not use it correctly. Either way, the glucose cannot get into the cells as it should. The energy they need stays outside the cell walls. And that is when the trouble starts.

A Breakdown of the System

Instead of going into the cells, the glucose keeps building up in the bloodstream. The high level of glucose in the blood sends a sort of alarm to the rest of the body. Too much glucose in the blood can make a person sick. The body needs to get rid of the extra glucose. To do that, the body makes large amounts of urine to flush the glucose out.

The cells, meanwhile, are slowly starving. They cannot get the glucose they need. The cells send an alarm, too. The body believes it is not getting food, and the person feels very hungry and eats more. But that just makes the problem worse. More and more glucose is in the blood but cannot help the cells. More and more urine is produced to flush out the glucose in the blood.

As time goes on, the body uses up most of its water producing urine. That makes the person very thirsty. And because no food is getting to the cells, the person feels very hungry, too. No matter how much a person with diabetes eats or drinks, it never seems to be enough. The problem gets worse and worse. The cells cannot do their jobs, and the body shuts down. Unless the person gets help immediately, he or she will die.

Not a Death Sentence

Today in the United States there are more than 16 million people who have diabetes. More than

An early diagnosis and proper treatment are the keys to successfully living with diabetes.

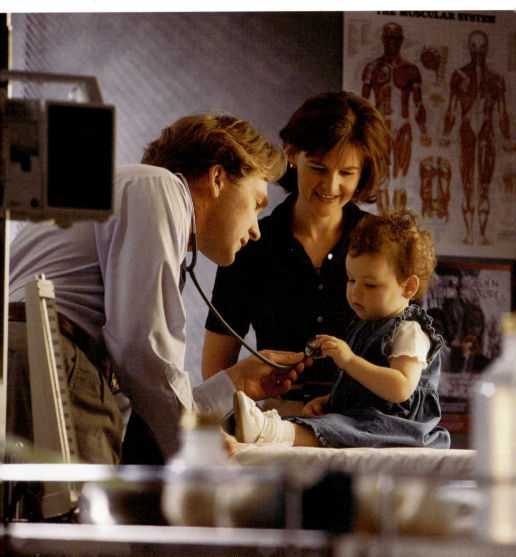

170,000 people each year die from diabetes, the third biggest killer after cancer and heart disease. However, even though diabetes cannot be cured, it can be controlled. **Diabetics** can live a normal life—if they are **diagnosed**.

That is the problem, say experts. Of the 16 million Americans who have diabetes, about 5 million do not realize it. People may have mild symptoms

Symptoms of Diabetes

- Excessive thirst
- Dry skin
- Slow-healing cuts
- Blurred vision
- Skin infections
- Numbness or tingling in feet
- Feeling hungry all the time
- Weight loss
- Feeling tired and weak
- Frequent urination
- Shakiness
- Dizziness

for years without being treated. That is dangerous, because glucose building up in the bloodstream can do lots of damage. It can affect the eyes, heart, lungs, and other organs. It can affect how the body heals cuts and sores.

"If you don't know you've got it, you can't treat it," says Vincent, whose father died of diabetes. "My dad probably had it for years, but didn't know. He felt okay. But inside, the glucose—the **blood sugar**—was making his heart weaker. He ended up having a heart attack, but it was caused by diabetes. All that time, he didn't know. And not knowing that killed him. This disease doesn't have to be a death sentence. But it sure can be if you're in the dark about it. Information—that's the best thing. You have to know how to take care of it."[2]

Being Smart

Charlie, a medical student, knows this is true. He found he had diabetes when he was in fifth grade. In the eleven years since then, he has been very active. He plays tennis and runs cross-country. He feels good, he says, but that is because he has learned how to control his diabetes.

"It's tough to hear you have diabetes," says Charlie. "I mean, it's a disease you'll be living with the rest of your life. When I found out I have diabetes, my doctor told me and my family that there was good news and bad news. I'll always remember

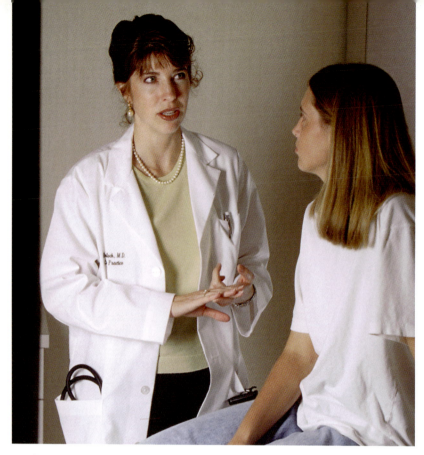

A doctor talks to a patient about the symptoms and treatment of diabetes.

how he said it, too. He said that the bad news is that you never get cured of it your whole life long. Till I'm an old man, I'll be diabetic. And the good news was that if I was smart about taking care of myself, I would *get* to be an old man!

"The best thing everybody can do is learn all they can about the disease. Every year, a lot of people find out they have it. But there are a lot who don't know what to look out for. Being smart about things like diabetes can save a life—maybe even your own."[3]

Chapter 2

A Different Way of Life

Diabetes is actually several diseases. The two which are most common are known as Type 1 and Type 2. Type 1 diabetes is most often found in children. Its symptoms are more severe. Type 2, which is the most common type of diabetes, is most common among adults. Both can be diagnosed with a test that shows how much glucose, or blood sugar, is in the bloodstream.

"I Panicked"

Sometimes people are frightened when they hear that they have diabetes. Pam, age twenty, did not know much about diabetes, but she knew it was serious.

"When the doctor told me, I panicked," she says. "I know you can't cure it, so I figured people died from it. I thought he was going to tell me I had six months to live or something. I started crying and everything. But really, once he explained things, I stopped feeling bad. Diabetes is a disease you have

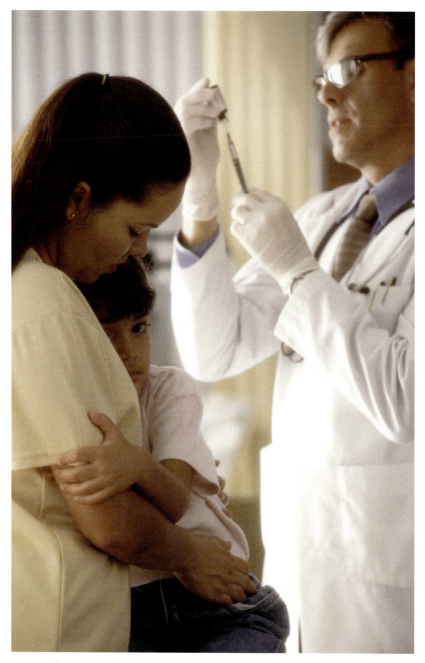

A mother comforts her child as a doctor prepares a shot. Children with diabetes learn to cope with the disease with help from their doctors and parents.

to manage. It's all about organizing yourself so you can deal with it. If you do, you'll be fine."[4]

Doctors explain to their patients that managing diabetes can be tricky at first. The first thing they talk about is keeping the blood sugar at a normal range. With too little or too much glucose in the bloodstream, the patient will be sick. That is the trick to managing diabetes—to keep the blood sugar at the right level.

Insulin for the Diabetic

Diabetics today are luckier than those born many years ago. Each day, they can give themselves the insulin their bodies do not produce. Scientists have found a way to make insulin that is very close to that made by a healthy pancreas. Most important, this insulin can do what natural insulin does—it can help the glucose get into the cells, to give them energy.

There is one drawback, however. Insulin cannot be taken in the form of a pill. Insulin that is swallowed would be digested, and the stomach acids would destroy its chemical makeup. The best way for insulin to get safely into the bloodstream is by an **injection**, or shot. Insulin injections are not usually given at a doctor's office. Instead, diabetics need to learn to give shots to themselves.

"That way, the patient is in charge of his or her disease," says one nurse. "Even children are taught how to give themselves injections. Someone might ask, 'Why can't my dad give me the shot?' The answer is simple—Dad or Mom may not always be around when you need a shot. You need to count on yourself."[5]

Diabetics give themselves insulin injections to help keep their blood sugar at a normal level.

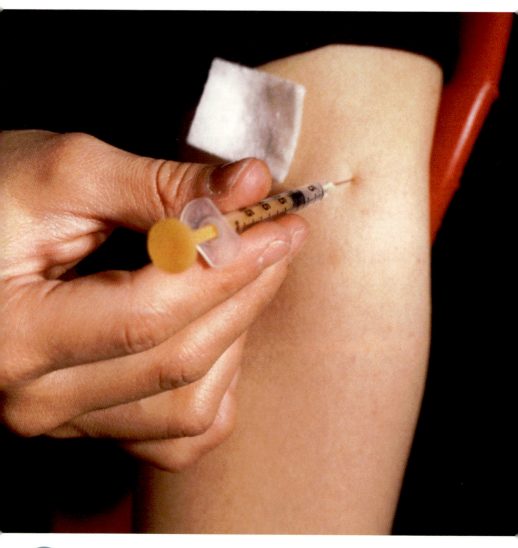

"I'm the Biggest Coward in the World"

Diabetics learn right away that the shot works best if injected into fat, rather than muscle. Injecting into fat is not as uncomfortable as into muscle.

Melanie, eighteen, was diagnosed with diabetes when she was eleven. She says that she dreaded the idea of giving herself a shot. However, she was surprised to find that it did not hurt much at all.

"I always hated any kind of shots," she says. "But these aren't like shots you get at the doctor. The needle is really, really thin, and it's coated with something that makes it go through the skin easier. I have to give myself two shots every day. I'm telling you, I'm the biggest coward in the world. But it's no big thing, really. And if I can do this, anyone can!"[6]

A Healthy Diet, Too

But diabetics need more than insulin to keep healthy. It is very important for people with diabetes to pay attention to the foods they eat. One reason, doctors have found, is that insulin seems to work better on a person who is not overweight. When insulin works well, the glucose goes from the blood into the cells. That means lower blood sugar, and that is a good thing.

The most important reason for diabetics to watch their diet has to do with blood sugar, too.

Many foods can raise the glucose levels too high. Foods high in oil or fat—salad oil, butter, and fried foods—can be a problem. Foods that are very sweet, such as desserts, candy, and soft drinks, will raise the blood sugar levels, too.

It is healthier for a diabetic to eat dairy products, eggs, and meat. But even these should make up only a moderate part of a person's diet. On the other hand, foods like fruits and vegetables are very good for a diabetic. So are carbohydrates, such as pasta and grains. These should make up the largest amount of the food a diabetic eats.

"The First Thing I Thought About"

Doctors know that a healthy diet usually means cutting back on foods people love. One woman says that when she found out she had diabetes, the thing that bothered her most was giving up desserts. "I've got a real sweet tooth," she says, "and I thought, 'Okay, that's the end of enjoyable eating. No more chocolate cake or stops at the ice cream store for me.'"[7]

In the past, doctors did tell their patients that they were not allowed to eat those foods. But changes like that are hard to make. A person is not likely to stay on a diet that is too rigid. Doctors understand that. That is why they try to be more flexible today.

Diabetics must be careful when making food choices. Too much junk food can lead to more serious problems.

"We don't say things like, 'You can never eat a piece of cake,'" says one nurse. "Even if we said it, no one would pay attention. So we say, 'Have a small piece.' It's all a matter of being aware of what you're eating."[8]

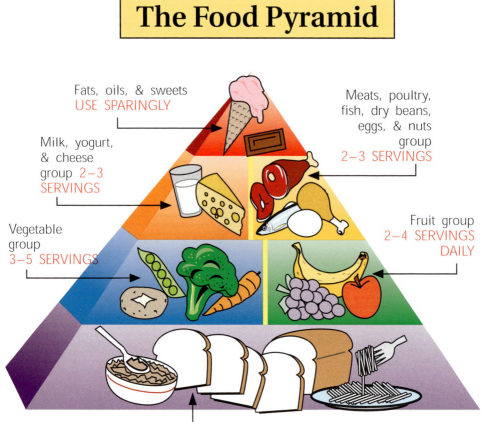

The Food Pyramid

Fats, oils, & sweets
USE SPARINGLY

Meats, poultry,
fish, dry beans,
eggs, & nuts
group
2–3 SERVINGS

Milk, yogurt,
& cheese
group 2–3
SERVINGS

Fruit group
2–4 SERVINGS
DAILY

Vegetable
group
3–5 SERVINGS

Bread, cereal, rice, & pasta group 6–11 SERVINGS

Source: The U.S. Department of Agriculture.

"It Forces Me to Stay Healthy"

Exercise is also important for good health. People with diabetes were once thought to be too frail to be active. Doctors advised their patients with diabetes to avoid exercising at all. However, that idea has changed. Research has shown two very important things happen when a person with diabetes exercises regularly.

The first is that exercise actually makes glucose levels in the blood go down. While a person is active, the body is burning glucose as fuel. Besides lowering blood sugar, exercise also strengthens the heart, lungs, and blood vessels. That is important because people with diabetes are at risk for having problems with their heart and lungs. By exercising, a person lowers that risk.

Diabetics who exercise regularly keep their blood sugar levels down and lower their risk of having heart and lung problems.

Exercise, a healthy diet, and insulin can allow diabetics to lead normal lives. "I can do anything," says Pam confidently. "I really believe that. I've had diabetes since I was in second grade. I play tennis, I swim, I even went mountain climbing last year!"[9]

Jeff, thirty, agrees. "In some ways, I've gotten better habits since I learned I have diabetes. I eat right. I make sure I exercise. I do those things because I have to. If I didn't have diabetes, I might get lazy with the diet. I might decide exercising is too much work. I could get away with that for awhile if I didn't have diabetes. But since I do, it forces me to stay healthy."[10]

Chapter 3

Living with Diabetes

L earning to live with diabetes is tricky at first. There are a lot of new things to get used to. Some people have trouble with the diet. Others have to work on exercising regularly. For many diabetics, it can be hard to adjust to being on a schedule. For instance, forgetting an insulin injection in the morning can cause high blood sugar later in the day.

Feeling Different

Doctors agree that diabetes is a difficult disease to manage during the teenage years. Teens want to feel more independent, but having diabetes gets in the way. Teens with diabetes often feel different from their friends. They have rules that other teens do not have.

Sometimes teens ignore the rules. They skip meals or eat things that they should not. Mary remembers that her son was very good at eating healthy foods at first. But when he turned thirteen, everything changed.

"He hit age thirteen and it was like he turned into a different boy," she says. "He let his diet go. I know he ate a lot of junk he wasn't supposed to. I'd find candy bar wrappers in his coat pockets. I would try and talk to him, but he wouldn't listen. It seemed like he'd rather risk his health just to be like all the other kids."[11]

Doctors understand how difficult it can be to have a serious disease like diabetes. They also know how dangerous it can be to ignore a good

Some teens join therapy groups to help them cope with the effects of diabetes.

diet or to forget an insulin injection. That is why many doctors assign a special counselor to work with younger patients. Having someone who understands what they are going through can make life a little easier for a diabetic.

Life's Emergencies

But even when diabetics try to follow the guide-lines, there can be trouble. Diabetics are at risk for health problems. Some are emergencies that can arise very quickly. Other problems are long-term. They may show up years later, but they can be life-threatening, too.

A very common emergency for diabetics is called **hypoglycemia**, or low blood sugar. It may sound strange that a diabetic could have *low* blood sugar. But there are many things that could cause it. An injection of too much insulin can cause the problem. Sometimes it can happen if a diabetic skips a meal or overexercises.

The symptoms of hypoglycemia may include shakiness, blurred vision, or dizziness. Sometimes the diabetic may feel confused or may have trouble remembering things. This can become an emergency very quickly. If the blood sugar drops too low, diabetics can black out, go into a coma, and even die.

Mike, fourteen, knows how he feels when his blood sugar is getting low. "I start getting really

An extreme rise or fall of a diabetic's blood sugar level can lead to a life-threatening emergency.

sweaty and kind of light-headed," he says. "It used to happen to me when I had gym class in the morning, and I hadn't had a good breakfast. I deal with it by always carrying some hard candy or a box of raisins in my backpack. That can raise my blood sugar to a safe level pretty quick."[12]

An emergency also can occur when blood sugar gets too high. This happens when a diabetic has gone several days without injections or paying attention to a healthy diet. This can be life threatening if it is not treated quickly. The warning signs are the same as the symptoms of diabetes. Sometimes the diabetic may also have stomach cramps or breathing problems. Usually a dose of insulin can help to handle this emergency.

Long-Term Problems

Diabetics are at risk for long-term problems, too, although these may not show up for many years. As mentioned earlier, diabetics are at risk for heart disease. They are also five times more likely to have a stroke than someone without diabetes.

One dangerous effect of diabetes is blockage in the large arteries. Blood cannot flow easily to the brain, heart, and other organs. When the brain cannot get the blood it needs, a person suffers a stroke.

Another long-term problem is eye damage. Just as the large arteries can become clogged, tiny blood vessels can be damaged, too. Excessive glucose in the blood can make the blood too thick for these blood vessels. Some of the tiniest blood vessels are located in the eyes. Ninety percent of people who have diabetes for twenty years or more will have blood vessel damage in their eyes. Some of the damage is severe, causing very blurry vision or even blindness.

Many diabetics suffer nerve damage, too. Nerves, which send and receive messages in the body, are surrounded by special cells. Too much glucose in the blood can seep into these cells, and that creates problems. These special cells get swollen and they squeeze the nerves. That means a person either feels a lot of pain or is numb and cannot feel anything at all.

Over time, diabetes damages the tiny blood vessels in the eyes. It is important for diabetics to have their eyes checked regularly.

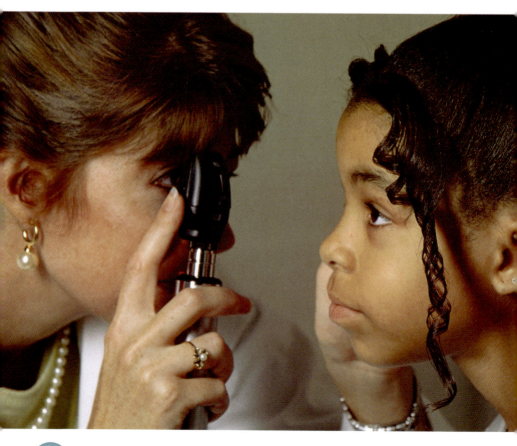

"I Couldn't Even Feel It"

When blood does not circulate as it is supposed to, cuts do not heal quickly. This is especially dangerous for a diabetic who has nerve damage. A person with nerve damage may not know that he or she has a cut. If the cut is on a foot, it might be even easier to miss. By the time the diabetic realizes there is a cut, it may be dangerously infected.

"That very thing happened to me," says Edgar, seventy. "I stepped on something, I guess. I couldn't even feel it, really. I've been kind of numb down on my feet for years. Anyway, the thing got infected. I didn't know it until the infection had gotten very bad. My foot got all swollen. I couldn't get my shoe on. That's when I figured it out. It was so bad, the doctor had to remove two of my toes."[13]

Monitoring Can Help

Doctors say that diabetics can prevent such problems by testing their blood sugar regularly. In the past, glucose tests could only be done in a doctor's office. But today diabetics are urged to test themselves.

The best way is to use a disposable **lancet**, a sharp blade, to prick a finger. The diabetic puts a single drop of blood on a special strip. The strip has chemicals which will make it turn colors, depending on how much glucose is in the blood. Knowing ahead of time that the level is too high or too low can prevent problems.

A group of children look on as a doctor uses a lancet to test a patient's blood sugar level.

"I have lancets and syringes with me all the time," says one girl. "I carry candy for emergencies. But my doctor also told me to wear a special ID bracelet. It has my name and also says that I have diabetes. If I am somewhere where no one knows me and I have a problem, the bracelet will alert people. It's something I wear all the time."[14]

Chapter 4

On the Horizon

It was 1921 when scientists first learned that a lack of insulin caused diabetes. In the years since then, amazing strides have been made in helping people with diabetes stay healthy. Some of these strides have been in making it easier and more convenient for diabetics to get the insulin they need.

New Ways to Get Insulin

Researchers have made a lot of progress with the **syringe**. Not long ago, syringes were made of glass and metal. The syringe lasted a long time, but it was inconvenient. After every use, it had to be boiled to keep it free from germs. Today most diabetics use syringes that are plastic. They are meant to be used only once and then thrown away. Diabetics say the plastic syringes were a real breakthrough.

"The glass one was what I started out with," says one diabetic. "It was a pain, too. No matter where I was, I was supposed to boil the thing down, and let it dry before putting it back in the leather case. It was such a bother. I was thirteen, I think, when I started with it. But there were a lot of times I didn't bother with a shot. Being over at somebody's house—it was such a production. It was embarrassing, so I would just take my chances."[15]

An even newer device for injecting insulin is a pen injector, so called because it looks just like a ballpoint pen. On the inside, however, it contains

The plastic syringe is one of the easiest and safest tools for injecting insulin.

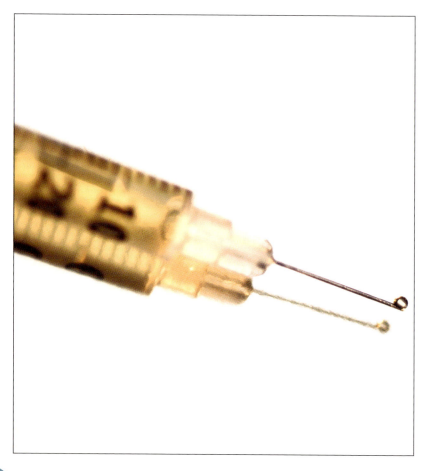

little cartridges of insulin, along with a needle. Because the insulin has been measured already, the diabetic does not need to fill the syringe.

Another new device is the jet injector. This is for people who do not want to use needles at all—even the ultrathin ones. The jet injector shoots the insulin so quickly that it acts like a liquid needle. The insulin can actually travel through the skin without a syringe.

The Insulin Pump

The insulin pump is another device for people who do not like to give themselves shots each day. It is a tiny computer, which a doctor implants under a diabetic's skin. Throughout the day, the pump releases drops of insulin at a steady rate.

Before patients with the pump do something that will raise their blood sugar, they can use a transmitter to signal the pump to change the dose of insulin. Every month the doctor can put new insulin in the pump.

No Needles

"My doctor told me that needles won't be used in the future," says one diabetic. "They're trying to come up with things that don't hurt at all, and are easy for people to use. I'd like that—I can't afford a pump. But I'd sure like to get away from syringes!"[16]

A doctor shows a patient how to use an insulin pump.

Scientists understand, and they are working on inexpensive ways to get insulin into the body—without needles. One possibility is making insulin thinner and lighter. Then it may be taken through an inhaler like a person with asthma might use. Another possibility is taking insulin into the body in a nasal spray. Researchers also are working on creating insulin in pill form. They are developing a special coating that can protect the insulin from stomach acids that would change its chemical makeup.

Pills might someday be an alternative to insulin injections.

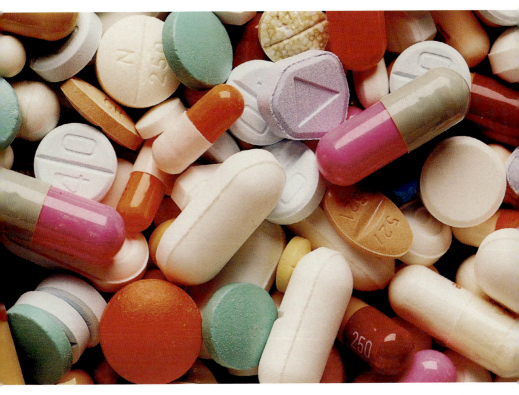

Some research also is being done on glucose testing to find ways to do it without needles. Scientists have been experimenting with a new monitor that looks like a wristwatch. It uses a tiny electrical current (instead of a needle) to see how much glucose is in the blood.

One doctor says that it is exciting to read about these new ideas. "You have to keep telling yourself that this stuff is real—or at least it will be very soon—and not out of a James Bond movie."[17]

Pancreas Transplants?

While some scientists are finding ways to make life easier for diabetics, others are trying to find a way to cure diabetes. So far, they have not found a cure. But some of their research shows promise.

One type of research has focused on **transplants**, or taking an organ from one person and putting it in another. Doctors have done surgery, putting a healthy pancreas in a person whose pancreas does not make insulin. The healthy pancreas comes from an organ donor. In some cases, the transplant is successful. The new pancreas makes insulin, and the person no longer has the symptoms of diabetes.

There have been some problems with this surgery, however. Often, the patient's body rejects the new pancreas. To prevent this, patients need to take strong drugs to help their bodies get used to the new organ. Unfortunately, those drugs can

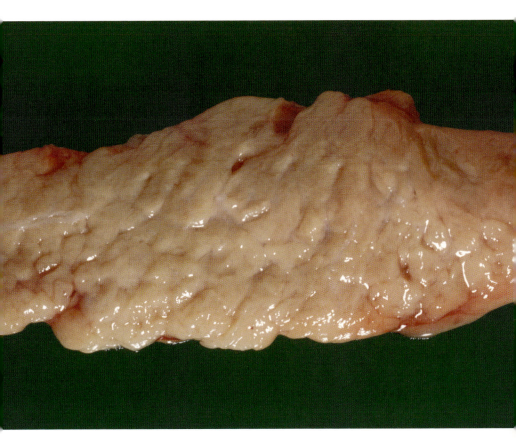

The pancreas provides insulin to the body. When it fails, a person becomes diabetic.

make the body weak. Patients are more likely to get sick from other diseases.

Cell Transplants

Some scientists have been trying a new idea in the past few years. Instead of transplanting a whole pancreas, they transplant certain cells from a healthy pancreas. About one teaspoonful of these cells is enough to start making insulin in the body.

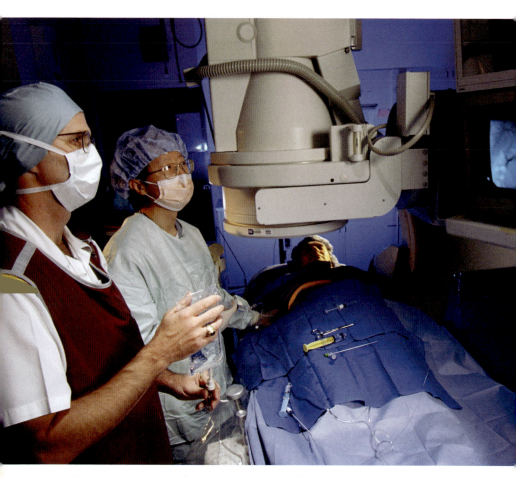

Surgeons transplant pancreas cells for the treatment of diabetes.

In 2000, doctors in Canada did cell transplants on seven patients. The patients soon found that they no longer needed insulin shots. The transplanted cells were making insulin, just as they were supposed to. After two years, six of those patients were still producing all the insulin their bodies needed. (The seventh needed less than half of the insulin he required before the transplant.)

A lot more study must be done to make sure the transplants are safe. Those patients who have had cell transplants are monitored carefully. Doctors want to be sure that no side effects occur. But for now, researchers are excited. The results have been promising so far, and more transplants are planned on other diabetics. Perhaps, say experts, cell transplants will someday cure every diabetic.

"A Good Time to Be Alive"

For now, diabetes remains a very serious disease. If it is not treated, it can lead to very serious problems. But it is a disease that can be controlled.

With proper treatment, diabetics can live happy, healthy, and normal lives.

"I figure a lot of it is in my hands," says one girl. "I can be smart or I can be dumb. If I'm smart, I'll test my blood sugar regularly. I'll eat right and exercise. Life isn't always easy being a diabetic. But I'm pretty confident.

"I think about kids like me who had diabetes a long time ago. They didn't have a chance. No one knew about insulin or what it could do. But today, we have it pretty good. Having diabetes, this is a good time to be alive!"[18]

Notes

Chapter 1: What Is Diabetes?

1. Personal interview, Charlie, July 18, 1998, Minneapolis, MN.
2. Telephone interview, Vincent, August 20, 2002.
3. Interview, Charlie.

Chapter 2: A Different Way of Life

4. Personal interview, Pam, July 21, 2002, Minneapolis, MN.
5. Telephone interview, Gloria, July 21, 2002.
6. Personal interview, Melanie, July 15, 2002, Richfield, MN.
7. Personal interview, Della, July 22, 1998, Minneapolis, MN.
8. Interview, Gloria.
9. Interview, Pam.
10. Telephone interview, Jeff, July 2, 1998.

Chapter 3: Living with Diabetes

11. Personal interview, Mary, August 1, 1998, St. Paul, MN.
12. Telephone interview, Mike, July 14, 2002.
13. Personal interview, Edgar, July 30, 2002, Eagan, MN.
14. Interview, Melanie.

Chapter 4: On the Horizon

15. Telephone interview, Jon, July 17, 2002.
16. Interview, Jeff.
17. Personal interview, Chris, August 12, 1998, Minneapolis, MN.
18. Interview, Pam.

Glossary

blood sugar: The amount of glucose in the bloodstream.

cell: The small structure that makes up the organs, blood, and bones of the body.

diabetes: A disease that occurs in people who cannot produce the insulin their bodies need.

diabetic: A person with diabetes.

diagnose: To study a patient's symptoms in order to determine what disease is causing them.

glucose: The natural sugar the body creates. Glucose is the body's main fuel.

hypoglycemia: Unusually low level of blood sugar.

injection: Another word for a shot. Diabetics give themselves injections of insulin.

insulin: A chemical that helps glucose get from the bloodstream into the cells.

lancet: A small, sharp blade used to prick a finger. Diabetics often use lancets when they test their blood sugar levels.

pancreas: An organ that is supposed to produce insulin.

symptom: An outward sign of a disease.

syringe: A device containing a needle used to give injections.

transplant: Surgically taking an organ from one person and putting it into the body of another person.

urine: The liquid waste produced by the body.

Books

Spike Nasmyth Loy and Bo Nasmyth Loy, *Getting a Grip on Diabetes: Quick Tips for Kids and Teens.* Alexandria, VA: American Diabetes Association, 2000. Written by two teenage brothers with diabetes, this is a very interesting book, especially for a young reader with the disease. Excellent tips for diabetic athletes, too.

Alicia McAuliffe, *Growing Up with Diabetes: What Children Want Their Parents to Know.* Hoboken, NJ: John Wiley and Sons, 1998. Very readable, with good section on the emotional aspects of having diabetes.

Linda O'Neill, *Having Diabetes.* Vero Beach, FL: Rourke Press, 2001. Good section on diagnosis and symptoms of diabetes. Very easy reading.

Alan Rubin, *Diabetes for Dummies.* Hoboken, NJ: John Wiley and Sons, 1999. Very good section on importance of diet for diabetics.

Websites

Children with Diabetes (www.childrenwithdiabetes. com). This website features nearly four hundred separate stories of teens and younger children with diabetes. The site includes photos as well as details about their lives with the disease.

Juvenile Diabetes Research Foundation International (www.jdrf.org). This site contains articles about medical strides in living with diabetes, interviews with famous athletes and celebrities who have diabetes, as well as a pen pal page for young people who have the disease.

Index

About the Author

Gail B. Stewart has written over ninety books for young people, including a series for Lucent Books called The Other America. She has written many books on historical topics such as World War I and the Warsaw ghetto.

Stewart received her undergraduate degree from Gustavus Adolphus College in St. Peter, Minnesota. She did her graduate work in English, linguistics, and curriculum study at the University of St. Thomas and the University of Minnesota. She taught English and reading for more than ten years. Stewart and her husband live in Minneapolis with their three sons.